THE LADIES CLUB

HEART-WARMING TALES FROM THE COUNTRY

THE COUNTRY LADIES CLUB

NERO ROSE

Blue

CONTENTS

PRAISE FOR NERO ROSE

"Lovely book on the friendships and goings on in small town New Zealand."

"These stories of country life in New Zealand are witty, funny, humorous, poignant—and very much a social commentary on the times we are living in."

"*The Country Ladies Club* is such a delight to read. The stories are authentically unique, told with both humour and depth, and rooted in lived experience. I am certain that anyone, wherever they are in the world, who is interested in tales from the heart will find joy in this collection of short stories.."

ABOUT THIS BOOK

Following the success of Book One, I am thrilled to share Book Two with you, my dear readers.

As you know, I consider myself a bit of a foodie. I love cooking, baking, and, most of all, sharing food with others. For me, there is nothing better than conversations held over a meal or a cuppa. With that in mind, I decided that Book Two would have a foodie theme.

We all have our stories of kitchen successes and kitchen disasters—I certainly do! So, in these pages, I'll be sharing both the triumphs and the mishaps for your enjoyment. After all, food and stories are always best when shared amongst friends.

I like to imagine my readers with a cuppa, or perhaps a glass of wine in hand, sitting back, relaxing, and having a laugh while they make their way through these tales.

Just like in Book One, each story in this collection stands alone. You can dip in and read them in any order that takes your fancy.

And remember—you are always welcome to share your stories with me too.

Here's to good food, good friends, and stories worth sharing.

FOREWORD: CASSANDRA THE JOYFUL ARTIST

Stories are like recipes. Each one carries its own flavour, a blend of humour, heart, memory, and meaning. Some are sweet, some are savoury, some may even leave a little after-taste of "oops"—but all are worth savouring.

When Nero Rose first shared her tales of the *Country Ladies Club*, I was immediately drawn in. Here was a collection of stories that celebrated the simple joys of friendship, food, and community—the kind of everyday magic that often gets overlooked. Book One was a feast of laughter and life lessons, told in Nero's warm and honest voice.

Now, in Book Two, she invites us back to the table—this time with a little extra spice. With a foodie theme, you can almost taste the stories as you read them. From kitchen triumphs to spectacular culinary flops, from fundraising fun to heartfelt community gatherings, every page reminds us that life, like cooking, is best when it's shared.

As The Joyful Artist, I know the value of creativity, connection, and joy in all their many forms. Nero captures that spirit beautifully. Her stories are more than entertainment; they're reminders that happiness is often found in the ordinary moments—cups of tea, shared meals, laughter around the table, and the courage to say yes to something new.

So settle in, pour yourself a cuppa (or a glass of wine), and let yourself be carried along by these tales. May you laugh, nod in recognition, and perhaps even be inspired to share your own stories too.

With joy,

Cassandra

The Joyful Artist

1

CARE BEARS

It's time I told you about the Care Bears. This is a small group within our Ladies' Club — a sort of subcommittee — whose role is to make sure that everyone in our community is being well looked after. As President of the Club, I of course sit on this very important little group, and sometimes I have to take the lead when chairing it, as not everyone is quite up to scratch with the level of leadership required. After all, every group needs a leader, and it may as well be me — that way I know things are being done properly.

So, what does "care" look like in our community? Well, it's about compassion and kindness, whether people are members of our club or not. We're a small rural community, and it matters that we look after one another. The Care Bears group has been a great success, helping people in all sorts of ways when there's been a need. Often this care takes the form of food, but there are plenty of other examples, too.

Take Joan, for instance — one of our oldest and most respected members. She and her husband, Joe, used to run a large sheep and beef station on the eastern side of the valley. These days, the physical work is beyond them, so the day-to-day running is in the hands of a capable manager and a small staff. Joan and Joe still take a keen interest in the business, and their sharp minds are highly valued by both staff and professionals alike. But Joan isn't as mobile as she once was, and being almost housebound is deeply frustrating for a woman used to being active at Club meetings and other community pursuits.

This is where the Care Bears step in. We set up a phoning roster so that someone checks in with Joan each day. A dozen wonderful members each take a turn, and although some calls stretch to thirty or forty minutes, they're always worthwhile. Joan is a treasure trove of wisdom and experience, and the ladies often come away uplifted themselves. I'm grateful to our members for this thoughtful act of care for such a special woman in our valley.

Food, of course, is another way we show care. A home-baked cake delivered to acknowledge a difficult time; a meal dropped off to a family with someone in hospital; a casserole for new parents. These gestures often lead to a cuppa and a good old chat, which lifts everyone's spirits. Sometimes the visit extends to small, practical tasks too: bringing in washing, folding laundry, or doing the dishes piled on the bench. Little acts of kindness can mean the world.

We also welcome new families to the valley with baking, or support those facing bereavement with meals. Sometimes it's a one-off gesture, sometimes it's ongoing. Whatever the circumstance, the truth is that we get back as much as we give.

At the moment, we've been supporting Trish and her husband, Colin, who run a large sheep station at the head of the valley. Trish is a long-time Club member, but we noticed she'd missed several meetings. On checking in, we discovered she was knee-deep in docking season. Normally, their son would come home to help, but like so many young Kiwis, he's overseas on his OE. Docking is a huge task — mustering, sorting, tagging, vaccinating — and all while keeping the household running and feeding the workers.

Trish is also the sort who's always helping others: she supports her daughter at the local salon, and she runs a boutique B&B in one of their cottages, actively involved in the owners' association. No wonder she hadn't made it down the valley lately. But that was our cue — she and Colin clearly needed some care themselves.

It only took a few phone calls. Within days, we had meals and baking organised, and two of us headed up the valley with boxes in hand. Trish and Colin were surprised — perhaps even a little overwhelmed — when we set the food on their table. I thought I saw a tear in Trish's eye.

"I never really knew what the Care Bears actually did," she admitted. "I've been too tied up with the farm, the B&B, and the salon to really think about it. But now I do understand. You'll see me putting my hand up to help, and I'll definitely be at the next meeting."

Colin smiled and added, "Yes, she'll be there. We'll make sure we organise the farm work around it. I can see it's too important to miss."

Moments like that are exactly why the Care Bears exist. Giving care binds us together as a community — and reminds us all that we are never alone.

In Longa Valley, care isn't just something we talk about — it's something we do, and in the giving we find ourselves richer too.

2

APRIL 1 MEETING

When your ladies' club meets on the first Tuesday of each month, it's inevitable that one day the date will fall on 1 April. That's exactly what happened earlier this year. What a memorable meeting it turned out to be.

Actually, I'm not so sure about the meeting itself, but the morning tea was unforgettable. I loved it, and I loved retelling it afterwards to my husband and friends. My kids tried to tell me I was childish, but I know that underneath their 'adult superiority' they were laughing too.

Let me share what happened at morning tea with the ladies of the Longa Valley Ladies' Club on Tuesday, 1 April. You can laugh or scoff — your choice!

Personally, I enjoy a little fun. So, when I was asked to "take a plate" to morning tea on April Fool's Day, I knew I had to add a playful twist. It didn't take long to decide I'd make chocolate lamingtons. I know they're really an Australian cake, but what the heck — let's have some fun with them.

I baked my sponge the day before, cut it into neat little

squares, and then inspiration struck. Out in the sleepout (now my art room!) I had some leftover squares of foam rubber from an old craft project. I held one against my sponge cake. Perfect! The height of the sponge and the foam rubber was almost identical. No one would know the difference — except me. I quickly cut a few foam squares to match.

The rest was simple. I whipped up some chocolate icing, dipped each cube in it, and then rolled it in coconut. They looked utterly convincing, lined up neatly on a plate to rest overnight. I went to bed smugly satisfied, already anticipating the mischief.

Morning came, and after tea and toast, I caught hubby and our son eyeing up the lamingtons. I warned them in no uncertain terms that touching my plate for the Ladies' Club would be the end of them. Luckily, I'd prepared extras — real ones — hidden in the fridge, which I planned to fill with cream later so the poor men had something to look forward to after fencing.

Before leaving, I added whipped cream to both the real lamingtons and the fakes — I'm not a total meanie after all. Then off I went to Bec's house for the meeting.

A few cars were already in the drive. I popped my plate on the big dining table among the wonderful spread of contributions — savouries, slices, biscuits, you name it. We ladies certainly know how to look after ourselves. Bec called out that the kettle was boiling, and soon we all had tea and coffee in hand.

It was warm enough to sit out on Bec's lovely deck. Conversation flowed, including a lively discussion about the upcoming duck-shooting season. Some moaned that their men were spending too much time building maimais and feeding up the ducks. I counted myself lucky my men weren't so interested.

When the food was served, I helped myself to a savoury fresh from the oven and one of the beautifully iced cookies. The savoury was delicious. But when I tried to bite into the cookie, I couldn't get my teeth through it.

I tried again.

Same result.

The icing was fine, but the biscuit itself tasted strange. Embarrassed, I glanced around. Marion and Pam also had iced cookies. They seemed to be struggling too.

Suddenly, Liz let out a dramatic shriek. She was jumping up and down, and Jane wiped her mouth, looking equally distressed. All eyes turned towards them. "It's the lamingtons!" Liz wailed. Marion and Pru, however, said theirs had been perfectly fine. My April Fool's trick had worked a treat.

Time to confess.

I raised my hand, grinning, and said, "Oops, sorry... April Fool's!" It took a moment for the penny to drop, then the whole group erupted into laughter. My little prank had gone down well.

Feeling emboldened, I mentioned the iced cookies. "Delicious icing," I said, "But impossible to bite through. Anyone else having trouble?"

Bec stepped forward sheepishly. "Guilty — well, actually, my kids are. They snuck into the kitchen this morning, iced a plate of dog biscuits, and made me promise to serve them. Then they dashed off to catch the school bus."

More hoots of laughter. It turned out I wasn't the only prankster. While I thought I was fooling the others, I'd been fooled myself.

Fair play all round. We had fun, shared some mischief,

and laughed until our sides ached. And of course, there was still plenty of truly delicious food to enjoy.

Then, with spirits high, it was time to get on with the monthly meeting of our Ladies' Club.

Another memorable morning with the Longa Valley Ladies' Club — full of fun, food, and just a little foolishness to keep us laughing until next time.

3

BYO BBQ FAMILY EVENING

If there's one thing we do well in Longa Valley, it's putting on a great family get-together. One of our most popular traditions is the annual post-Ag Day barbecue. It's become a joint effort between the Ladies' Club and the School PTA, and after a few years, it now feels almost as important as Ag Day itself. In fact, it's nearly worth all the stress of Ag Day just to enjoy the follow-up BBQ where everyone lets their hair down.

Anyone who has been involved in a rural school will know the stresses of Pets' Day, Calf and Lamb Day, or Ag Day — the name might differ, but the principles have been the same for generations all over New Zealand. On top of the animals, there are all the extra activities to add to parents' headaches: flower arranging, fruit and vegetable characters, sand saucers, art projects, baking projects... and the list goes on. I'm sure you get the gist, so I won't dwell on the dreaded day itself.

Well, actually, I will share just one wee story before I get back on track. A few years ago, while I was on the Board of Trustees at Longa Valley School, we welcomed a new principal. He was a lovely man with excellent references, but he was straight out of the city — too tempting a target for us rural folk. We solemnly informed him that, as Principal, he was required to wear a white lab coat and carry a clipboard on Ag Day. He took us at our word. His poor wife even had to source the coat. On the day, he turned up looking exactly as instructed. It was hilarious but very naughty of us, and needless to say, the lab coat and clipboard lasted all of two minutes.

Back to the point — we're good at family social events here in the valley, and what better excuse to celebrate than the end of Ag Day. A few years ago the Ladies' Club suggested to the PTA that we all wind down with a BBQ and some family games. The idea stuck and has since become an annual highlight.

By now, we've perfected the formula. The school grounds and facilities make the perfect venue. Families bring along their meat to cook on the BBQs, a salad for the communal table, their own drinks, and their plates and cutlery. The Ladies' Club takes care of set-up, provides a few extra salads and desserts, and always ensures there are ice creams for the children. We also organise a few games.

It's heart-warming to see families gathered on the school playground having good old-fashioned fun. You may scoff, but sack races, egg-and-spoon races, and wheelbarrow races never lose their charm. We run them in age groups, but the most competitive — and the most entertaining — are always the adults, especially the dads. It's a joy to see them forget the pressures of farm and work life, competing like kids. The children, of course, love it most of all, watching their mums and dads joining in.

While the races are going on, some of our ladies set up the tables with salads and help the men behind the BBQs.

Once the grills are going and the air is filled with the unbeatable smell of barbecued meat, families gather in the courtyard. The dads get stuck into cooking, the mums sort out the salads and plates, and soon everyone is tucking in. I love looking around to see families on picnic blankets, happily sharing their meals.

And then the peace is broken — Rita arrives.

Now, you need to know a little about Rita before she bursts onto the scene. She's been a Ladies' Club member for years and has firmly established herself as the "busiest person in the district" — possibly in all New Zealand. What that really means is she spends a lot of time telling everyone how busy she is, without ever saying exactly what she's busy doing. She does help on the farm, but apparently, she's too busy to do too much of that either.

She is also never, ever on time. We long ago learnt to give her an earlier start time so that she might just arrive only thirty minutes late. Still, we all love her, quirks and all. She's entertaining, always full of stories (relevant or not), and best of all, she's a marvellous baker. Her still-warm-from-the-oven contributions are legendary.

So, when Rita roars up in her ute, slams on the brakes, and strides out — empty-handed — we all look up. She's missed the memo about bringing her own meat and salad, of course. Without hesitation, she heads straight for the BBQs. "Ooh, look at that, a beautiful piece of steak cooked perfectly. Just what I need after the busy day I've had!" And before Paul can even blink, she's carving into his sirloin — the one he'd been looking forward to all day. The look on his face was priceless. Everyone had seen and heard Rita claim her prize, and though we felt sorry for Paul, no one was entirely surprised. That's Rita for you. Most disappointing of all, she hadn't even brought her usual baking to soften the blow!

The evening finished with a final group challenge I'd read about from a youth event. Teams of ten — six kids and four adults — had five minutes to create the longest possible line using only themselves and what they had on them. The results were hilarious: long lines of hair ties, belts, hankies, wallets, glasses, coins, phones, shoes, and even shirts. The dads, naturally, got very competitive. Soon, people were stretching out across nearly the entire rugby field. It took just as long afterwards to gather everything up and return it to the right owners, but what fun it was.

Once again, the Ladies' Club and PTA could feel proud of another successful community event. Everyone went home tired but happy, the children worn out and — with luck — sleeping in the next morning, giving their deserving parents a little more rest.

In true Longa Valley style, we ended the night with full bellies, tired children, and plenty of laughter — another reminder that when our community comes together, we always go home richer in spirit.

4

DINNER OUT

As I've mentioned before, I do have a life outside of the Ladies' Club. This story isn't strictly about the Club — though the women involved later became members.

A couple of years ago, a new principal arrived at Longa Valley School. You may have read about him in another tale. He came with an excellent reputation from his city school, and we were delighted to welcome him into our rural community. Trevor was keen to get involved, and his wife, Tina, quickly became active too. She joined in local events and supported Trevor at school functions.

One day at the store, Tina invited Peter and me to dinner at their place on Saturday night. It was such a lovely invitation that I accepted at once — hoping Peter hadn't already earmarked the evening for a rugby test or something similar. Tina added that she was also asking Elaine and Mike to join us. Apparently, she loves entertaining and finds that three couples make for the perfect evening.

Naturally, Elaine and I compared notes. Yes, we had both received our invitations. And yes, both Peter and Mike were hesitant. Socialising with the school principal and his wife wasn't their idea of a relaxing Saturday night. Our husbands are dyed-in-the-wool rural blokes: happiest at home, feet up, beer in hand, rugby on the telly. Elaine and I agreed that the men were as bad as each other, but an evening out would do them good. It was time they ironed a decent shirt and joined in.

Saturday dawned bright and sunny. I dropped some bits and pieces off at the school, where a few parents were busy with a painting bee. As I headed back to the car, Tina called me over.

"Just checking you're all set for tonight," she said. "I've got the menu under control, and you'll love the three-course meal I'm preparing. It's been wonderful getting out my best dinner set and silver service again since our move here. I do hope Elaine and Mike understand that when I entertain, I like to do it properly."

"Lovely to see you, Tina. Yes, we're all looking forward to tonight. It does sound like you're going to a lot of trouble for us. We're just ordinary folk, so please don't do too much. See you around six."

I took a deep breath in the car. That had sounded like a gentle warning about her expectations for "good behaviour". Elaine and I could manage — we know how to play ladies when the occasion calls for it — but Peter and Mike were another matter. I phoned Elaine, and we decided to give our men a heads-up. They'd need to play nicely, as Trevor and Tina were still new to the district.

When I relayed Tina's words to Peter, he screwed up his nose. Not a good sign. Soon, he was on the phone to Mike. From the nodding, umming, chuckling, and laughter, it was clear there was some scheming going on. Elaine and I had to intervene quickly before the plotting got out of hand. Between us, we reined them in, reminding them that Trevor and Tina might do things differently, coming as they did from the city, and that we ought to help them settle in gently.

That evening, the four of us dressed in our best clothes and travelled together from Elaine and Mike's. We were warmly greeted at the door by Trevor, who told us Tina would be down in a minute.

Mike presented a newspaper parcel, greasy and crumpled like a takeaway bundle. With a hearty chuckle, he announced, "Brought something along to help out, seeing as there are a lot of mouths to feed tonight."

Tina swept into the room, every inch the gracious hostess, and accepted the parcel with a smile. Inside was nothing more than a fresh loaf of bread. "Thank you, Mike," she said smoothly. "I didn't have bread on the menu, so perhaps you're right — this will fill the gap." One point to Tina for her quick wit. I was impressed she took it all in stride.

We moved into the dining room and began with pea and ham soup. Conversation was a little stiff at first, but Mike's bread went down well and seemed to put him in his place. Soon the wine was flowing, Tina brought out the main course, and things warmed up. The talk loosened, and we found ourselves making connections — shared interests, common friends from years ago.

By dessert, the awkwardness had melted away. The men, once so wary of Trevor, were deep in chat about rugby and cricket. I even heard whispers of a fishing trip in the planning.

So much for our clever-clogs husbands and their suspicion of "city slickers". All it took was good food and a shared evening, and three couples found themselves at the start of new friendships.

That evening proved what we often forget — sometimes all it takes is sitting around the same table to realise how much we truly have in common

5

MEN'S OOPSIES

We had a great session where we all shared our kitchen oopsies. If laughter is the best medicine, we all got some great doses of some really good medicine from that session.

After the sharing of the stories we had our coffee and chat. The funny thing is that theme of oopsies carried on but with a slightly different theme. The ladies mentioned that their men had some oopsies that they felt were stories to be told. Some of those stories are also worthy of sharing so let's put them together now and enjoy.

I recalled a memory from many years ago relating to my own Dad. Back in the day, my mum did some part-time work for a caterer. This was mostly weekend evenings helping with the catering at weddings, family celebrations and other community events.

On some occasions, there would be some food left over, and usually the caterer would tell Mum to take some home. While I said it was leftover food, it was really best described as food scraps, and therefore became food for our pigs.

Occasionally, we, the family, did get to benefit from some leftover food that was more fit for human consumption!! There was a Sunday morning when Mum got up quite late after having worked into the wee hours of the morning completing a catering job.

When she came out to the kitchen, she reached up for something on top of the fridge. There was nothing there. Where was that tin she had left there when she had arrived home? Was that the tin with some food in it? Apparently, it was. There was one person who knew where said tin was now.

Dad.

I think he clicked very quickly that something was amiss as he quietly said, "I thought that was another offering for the pigs so I gave it to them earlier with their other scraps."

There was silence.

"That was some of the absolutely beautiful Sweet and Sour Pork from yesterday's wedding reception. That was going to be a very nice Sunday lunch."

I have no idea what we actually had for lunch, but it certainly wasn't Sweet and Sour Pork.

Marion had a story to tell about her uncle Ron. Ron and his wife, Mary farmed on a very remote property at the end of a valley on the other side of Silverton. Neither of them went to town very often as they were very happy living on their isolated block and being as self sufficient as they could.

There would be times when one of them did need to go to town, so they would toss a coin to see whose turn it was. On this particular occasion, Ron had lost the toss and so it was his turn to head to town to complete the necessary chores.

As was his custom, he called around to their friends, Lorna and Steve's place at lunch time. Always keen for a bit of a free feed, Ron turned up on the doorstep. This time, there was no one at home, but the back door was open, so Ron carried on inside.

He decided that he could help himself to lunch as it appeared that Lorna had left some soup on the stove. He enjoyed that help yourself meal, tidied up, and then left to head back to town to complete the chores before heading back home.

Nothing special about that story, you may say.

Wrong.

That was part one. Part two happened a few months later on Ron's next trip to town. This time, Lorna and Steve were home when Ron called, hoping to get some lunch. He sat at the table and went on to say, "Hope you guys didn't mind me calling in last time I was in town. You weren't home, but I came in anyway and helped myself."

"It doesn't surprise me that you came in and helped yourself, but I never saw any evidence that you had been," said Lorna.

"Well, I must have cleaned up good. I was just lucky that you left that really nice pearl barley soup on the stove. All I had to do was heat it up, fill a bowl, enjoy it, then put everything away. Bloody good soup that was too, by the way."

"Pearl barley soup. Mmmm. I haven't made pearl barley soup for a very long time. Are you sure? I just can't remember making any soup really. Tell me more, as it just doesn't sound right."

"I tell you, it was. Big pot on the stove. Pearl barley on the top, but when I heated it up and stirred it all up, it was a great mixture. Very tasty. Did me for a good feed on a town day."

Steve looks up from his paper. "I know what he's talking about. That was the pot of chook scraps I had cooked up. Might have forgotten about it for a day or two. Might have got a bit fly blown. Oh shit. That's what you had for lunch, Ron, you silly old bugger."

It took us all a while to recover from that story.

After a time, we were ready for Sally to share her story about her husband. It was a few years ago, and Sally and Aaron were new parents. There was so much excitement as this was their first baby and the first grandchild for both sets of grandparents. It was only right to celebrate with a special baby naming ceremony.

Family and friends were all invited to join them for the ceremony, followed by afternoon tea. Sally had very proudly made a special celebration cake. The plan was to ice and decorate it the night before so that everything would be all ready for the big day. It was good to be organised a bit ahead of time with a young baby to consider as well.

Sally settled baby Rebecca for the night. She then went to grab the cake container and begin her icing and decorating project. She took the cake out and put it on a serving plate. But wait. Were her eyes deceiving her? Was there really a corner piece cut out of the cake? Was it no longer a complete, whole, square cake? Oh dear. She may or may not have sworn out loudly.

She may have made enough noise to get Aaron's attention. "What's wrong? I only had a small piece!"

How could he? Obviously, there was a communication breakdown over a vital piece of information. It was certainly a time that called for calm. You know, count to 10, then start again.

Luckily, Sally managed that and found her way through with a plan. She would cut along the line of the piece that Aaron had taken, and then the finished product would be a rectangular cake rather than the original square cake. Not perfect, but at least what started as a problem was resolved. Who would ever know that that beautiful cake was plan B.

Aaron did feel a bit guilty about the demise of plan A being his doing, but was so proud of Sally and the total success of plan B. As he stood there with Rebecca in his arms, he couldn't have felt better about how his life was these days. A beautiful and clever wife, a gorgeous baby, and a uniquely special celebration rectangular cake.

Seems like the perfect ending to this story about men's oopsies, but I need to tell you that there are plenty of other stories in the store cupboard ready to roll out sometime in the future.

In Longa Valley, whether it's the ladies or the men, there's never any shortage of stories to keep us laughing — and that's what makes our community so very special

6

IF YOU'VE GOT IT, USE IT

Many moons ago, when I was helping at a youth group camp out near Lake Ellen, we had a late-night visit from a couple of policemen. If things were quiet in town, they sometimes came out to the lake to check on things, as it was a popular spot for dumping cars and other mischief. They were happy to stop and chat with us adults as we enjoyed a late supper after a long day wrangling energetic young people.

As they were about to leave, one of them asked if there was anything they could do for us. I cheekily replied, "Well, you could get all those young ones to go to sleep for us."

His answer: "If you've got it, why not use it!"

With that, they drove quietly over to the accommodation block, flicked on their blue and red lights, gave a quick blast of the siren, and then, over the loudspeaker, came the booming voice of authority:

"Would all the members of the Longa Valley Youth Group please go to sleep now."

Magic.

Silence.

We didn't hear a peep from them until 7:15 the next morning.

Over the years, I've often remembered those words: If you've got it, why not use it!

It got me thinking — what do we have in our community that we could use, not just for ourselves but for the benefit of our Ladies' Club and the wider district? Clearly, we no longer had policemen on call with sirens and loudspeakers, but we had plenty of other resources close at hand.

At our next meeting, I shared my idea. "I've been thinking about that saying, 'If you've got it, why not use it.' And I couldn't help but notice that many of us have citrus trees. Every year, fruit drops to the ground, wasted. I know I'm guilty of it, and I've seen plenty of others with oranges and lemons rotting under the trees. Why not do something about it? Why not use it?"

Hands shot up everywhere. Ideas flew thick and fast:

- Fresh juice
- Frozen juice and ice blocks
- Fresh fruit
- Candied peel
- Baking with fruit
- Dehydrated fruit
- Preserves
- Marmalade

Pam, never short on suggestions, piped up: "Why don't we have a Ladies' Club stall at the school Ag Day next month?"

Trish was quick to agree — and to everyone's surprise, she even offered to coordinate. Usually, she was one of the hardest to draw in, so this was a breakthrough. "I always feel guilty about the wasted citrus at my place," she confessed. "I can provide plenty of fruit, but I'm hopeless at turning it into anything. I'll happily organise things though."

With such enthusiasm, we knew we had to go for it. Plans were made, rosters sorted, and soon we were in full action mode.

When Ag Day arrived, I couldn't have been prouder. Our stall looked amazing. Children had helped gather fruit and even created colourful posters. Our jam experts had filled jars with golden marmalade. Others had baked cakes and muffins bursting with citrus flavour. On a warm day, the freshly squeezed orange juice was a huge hit. Thirsty parents and visitors couldn't resist stopping for a glass — and while they were there, many picked up a jar of marmalade or a slice of cake to take home.

By the end of the day, we were exhausted but elated. The project had been a triumph. We had worked together, contributed to the school's annual event, provided treats for the community, and raised funds, too. The ladies voted to split the profit: half to the school, to be spent as they saw fit, and half to our Club, earmarked for the "Oldies' Christmas Party" we hold each year.

As I looked around at our happy, tired team, I thought back to that policeman's words. If you've got it, why not use it? We certainly had — and the whole community was better for it.

That's the Longa Valley way — turning what we have into something worth sharing, and always coming out richer together.

7

FOOD FOR GOOD

They say the way to a man's heart is through his stomach. I'd go further: the way to anyone's heart is through their stomach. Food isn't just nutrition — it's comfort, kindness, and often the simplest way to show we care. Our Ladies' Club has plenty of stories to prove it.

Over the generations, our strength has always come from coming together to provide food for others. Those who receive it find strength in knowing they are supported, while those who give feel just as rewarded.

As President of the Ladies' Club, I'm often the first point of contact when food is needed. Let me share some times when our ladies worked their magic with food.

A couple of years ago, there was a major earthquake on the east coast, badly affecting families around Papawai. Once I heard how serious it was, I rang Jane. Soon enough, we were all on the phones, arranging to meet at Lottie's Kitchen to plan. We've learned over the years that good planning always works better than rushing in with a knee-jerk reaction. We asked the right questions: What are the real needs? Do they have power? Can they stay in their homes?

By the time we gathered at Lottie's Kitchen, we had more information. Coffees ordered, pens and paper ready, we sat around the long table listing ideas. Ready-to-eat food was top priority. Some volunteered to cook meat. Others donated sausages, chops, and patties from their freezers. Sally rang in from the supermarket to say they'd donate twenty loaves of bread. Within two hours, we had a list of food, donors, and tasks.

I rang my nephew, a helicopter pilot. Thankfully, his boss agreed to fly in the donations. The only condition was that we had to be ready by midday the next day.

So the Ladies' Club went into top gear. Cakes went into ovens, oranges were picked, cupboards were cleared of spares, and boxes were filled with tins of food, fruit, crockery, glasses, and even toilet paper. Peter rolled his eyes at my stockpile of loo rolls, but for once it came in handy!

By 12.30 pm the helicopter was loaded: frozen meat, fresh baking, cooked meals, fruit, bread, bottled water, and even spare plates and bowls to replace the ones lost in the quake. Ben strapped it all in and lifted off. At Papawai, he was met by the local Ladies' Club, who happily took charge of distributing everything. More deliveries followed in the weeks ahead. And we all knew — one day it might be our turn to need the same kind of help.

Closer to home, we do the same for families in need. Right now, we're providing meals for the Barnes family. Their six-year-old is in the hospital long-term. Mum, Jenny, stays at the hospital while Dad, Charlie, keeps working as a farm manager and caring for their two older children. The kids are sensible, but life is still a juggle. So we deliver hot meals, or sometimes several frozen ones at once. Whoever drops off food also folds washing, does dishes, or whatever else is needed. Fish pies, mac'n'cheese, lasagnes, meatloaves — we make sure they're looked after.

Not every effort goes smoothly. Marion once came home from the hospital after surgery, and we clubbed together to provide meals. Sally made chicken lasagne, I made cottage pie, and Linda made one of her special fish pies. Linda delivered them, but when no one answered the door, she left the dishes at the back. Unfortunately, Marion's husband, Jim, came home just as the dogs discovered the parcels. By the time he reached the doorstep, the food was gone and the culprits were back in their kennels licking their chops.

Marion debated whether to confess at all, but honesty won. At the next meeting, she returned the dishes and, red-faced, told us what had happened. There were gasps at first, then giggles, then outright laughter. Poor Marion and Jim missed out on the food, but the story itself fed us all for weeks afterwards.

Time and again, food has proven to be the special ingredient. It nourishes, comforts, and connects us — body and soul.

8

DEATH BY CHOCOLATE

I've just returned from a lovely week away with my sister, Jenny, down south. Each year, we try to spend a few days together. Sometimes we meet in a different town if there's a show or exhibition to see, other times we stay at each other's homes. This year it was my turn to visit her. As the years pass, we've realised how important it is not to let life's busyness get in the way of family.

As luck would have it, Jenny's garden club was meeting during my visit. I thought it would be fun to go along — something different for me, and a chance to meet her friends and neighbours.

Before we left, Jenny did a quick lap of the garden, gathering a basket of blooms, two cauliflowers, and some lemons. I noticed some empty green glass bottles like the ones Peter uses for his home brew. Jenny explained that those were the club's chosen display vessels for competitive blooms.

We arrived at the rugby club hall where the meeting was held. The place was already buzzing. Jenny set her cauliflower on the vegetable table, the lemons on the fruit table, and then fussed over which flowers were worthy of being staged in the green bottles. I couldn't believe how seriously she — and everyone else — took the business of choosing and placing blooms.

A bell rang, signalling five minutes to meeting time. Suddenly, the room hushed as everyone took their seats. Madam Chair opened proceedings, introducing me as Jenny's visiting sister. My attention wandered a little until I noticed two women with clipboards circling the display tables. Then the announcement came:

"Judging is complete. Let's move to the tables for the results."

I dutifully followed. The judges offered feedback: "Check petals carefully. Some blooms had tears or flaws. Watch out for insects hiding on the undersides — black bugs cost a few marks."

This went on longer than I expected, but the members nodded and agreed with every word. At the end, applause rang out for the winners. Jenny was thrilled to come third overall — her cauliflower was declared "perfect." Ten out of ten!

On the way home, she explained that while the club was friendly and informal, the competitions had been running monthly for over twenty years. Members valued them dearly.

It reminded me of the trophies tucked away in a suitcase at Jane's place. They hadn't been used for over a decade. Once upon a time, they were awarded monthly for best bloom, best biscuit, best buttonhole, best knitted peggy square, and so on. No wonder enthusiasm waned. But why not bring them back in a new way?

So at our next Ladies' Club meeting, I presented my idea: an annual competition day with trophies awarded to the winners. The competitions would be themed and fun. We brainstormed ideas: Tea for Two, Couple's Cuppa, Smoko Tray, Breakfast in Bed, Supper Special, and finally Death by Chocolate.

No surprise, Death by Chocolate won the vote.

The rules were simple: each entry to include a plate of three chocolate-based food items (homemade or commercial), a decorated chocolate fish (we'd supply those), and a decorated chocolate box (competitor's choice of size and shape).

Now all that remains is for Jane to polish the trophies and for me to re-read my Chocolate Therapy book. I plan to bring along a few boxes of chocolates to add some hilarity with a surprise therapy session at the end. Those always go down well — laughter, personality insights, and more than a little indulgence.

The funniest part? I don't even like chocolate. But the joy it brings to others is enough to make me look forward to our Death by Chocolate competition.

Sometimes the sweetest moments aren't about the chocolate at all, but the laughter it melts into.

9

KITCHEN OOPSIES

We love having a guest speaker at our Ladies' Club meetings. It's a great way to learn new things, get upskilled, and broaden our horizons. But there are times when we don't have a guest speaker, and on those days we enjoy each other's company instead. We learned long ago that it's best to have a theme to guide our discussions — otherwise the danger is we slip into gossip. You know the kind: everyone leaning in to hear about people they don't particularly love. That's not us.

Last month was one of those guest-speaker-free days, so I chose the theme Kitchen Oopsies. The giggles around the room told me we were in for a treat. I knew we'd leave that meeting smiling and bouncing home with laughter in our hearts.

To get things rolling, I shared my own tale. Years ago, when I was newly pregnant and rather hormonal, we had a cousin's wedding five hours away. I decided a bacon and egg pie would be perfect picnic food.

What I didn't realise was that the pastry on the bottom had a hole. The pie went into the oven looking perfect. But when I peeked in later, there it was: a bacon pie on the rack and one enormous blob of cooked egg bubbling on the oven floor. I cried and cried. My husband was no help, just shaking his head in disbelief. I packed the so-called "pie" anyway and made him eat it on the road. By the time the wedding was over I'd recovered, but you can be sure I've checked the bottoms of my pies very carefully ever since.

Bec was next. She remembered being a new wife determined to fill the cake tins. She baked a batch of sultana biscuits. They looked fine in the oven. They even looked fine out of it. But one bite proved they were as hard as concrete. Furious at the waste of good sultanas, she sat for nearly an hour smashing the biscuits just to rescue them.

At the end she had a jar of what she proudly called "pre-cooked sultanas." Her husband, Chris, came home, popped one in his mouth, and declared she should take them back to the supermarket for a refund. Needless to say, the jar went the same way as the crumbs — straight into the bin.

Sally piped up next. She was a new bride at the time, desperate to impress her in-laws, Joan and Joe. She baked what was meant to be a Never Fail Chocolate Cake. Well, Sally proved that label wrong. The cake was such a disaster she tossed it to the birds and quickly baked another.

The problem was that the birds wouldn't touch it either. They pecked, hopped back, and flew off in disgust. Mortified, Sally fished it back out of the yard and buried it in the bottom of the rubbish bin before her in-laws arrived. Luckily, her second cake was perfect, and Joan and Joe never knew.

Marion followed with a story that wasn't really about cooking at all. She had her parents up for a Sunday lunch. Dessert was simple: ice cream and fruit salad. While her husband fetched the ice cream, Marion opened the tin labelled fruit salad — only to find baked beans. Embarrassed, she quickly swapped to a tin of apricots and saved the day.

Later, she emailed the manufacturer, who sent a profuse apology and vouchers. But weeks later, she opened a tin of corn to make fritters and found peaches inside! That's when she remembered her Aunty's hen's night present: a box of cans with steamed-off labels glued back on randomly. The mystery was solved, and Marion never did get around to sending that second email.

Finally, Jane shared her infamous birthday cake fail. For her husband Stu's milestone party, she baked his cake late at night — and promptly fell asleep. The smell of smoke woke her hours later. The cake was charcoal. She tossed it to the chooks, thinking no one would know. But during the party, Stu pulled out a parcel wrapped in newspaper and said in his speech:

"I thank Jane for being my constant through the years. But I'm going to expose her secret tonight. Open this parcel."

Gasps echoed as the charred cake was revealed. Jane owned up, red-faced, before revealing she'd already baked a fresh, beautifully decorated replacement. The guests enjoyed every bite — along with the story.

By the time we'd heard everyone's tales, we agreed that no guest speaker could have beaten our own members that day. We finished with afternoon tea, still chuckling, and swapping yet more kitchen oopsies that will no doubt resurface at another meeting.

Because sometimes the sweetest memories are baked not from perfection, but from the oopsies we laugh about together.

10

SORRY JILL

We're very proud of our community dinners, which we put on three times a year for the ladies of Longa Valley and the surrounding areas. The idea began when we were considering ways of including more women in our Ladies Club. We wanted to encourage women to get out for an evening every now and then and share some time with others. The men and children can surely be left at home to take care of themselves occasionally. The women deserve some time to themselves – to talk, share a meal and a drink, and listen to interesting guest speakers. And so, our Ladies' Dinners were born.

Those first couple of dinners were actually hard work for the ladies of our club. We had to plan a menu, work together in the kitchen to cook the food, set up the Golf Club Lounge where we held the evenings, and then serve up the meal. Of course, just like at home, there were the dreaded dishes to deal with afterwards as well. It was difficult for the Ladies Club members to find any time to relax, catch up with friends, or sit and enjoy the guest speaker. In a way, the very purpose of the evening was being lost for those of us delivering it.

It was, however, a good exercise in teamwork. Everyone had a role to play. Some people donated food, and these donations really guided what our menu would be. We could then work towards creating a delicious two-course meal for the ladies who came to join us. Along the way, I think we all picked up new ideas and tips as each person added their own slant on how to do things. You can probably imagine that some of our planning and preparation times were quite lively. The best part was that the end results were always worthwhile and much appreciated by all who attended.

Of course, we had to do this properly. Some members took responsibility for setting up the tables and the Golf Club Lounge we used as our venue. Becky was a whizz at creating beautiful floral table centrepieces which were always admired. We all collected the right fish tins that she liked to use for these arrangements. My family enjoyed a couple of smoked fish pies so I could donate the tins for Becky's creations. It made everything feel just that bit more special to have such a thoughtful finishing touch.

The food was set out buffet-style, and there was always plenty for those who fancied second helpings. There were never too many leftovers, so I think we did well on the catering front.

Following the meal, tea or coffee was served so everyone could sit back and enjoy the guest speaker. We learned such a wide range of things at those sessions – from new coastal cycleways and river clean-up projects to hearing from stall-holders at the Silverton Farmers' Market. The question-and-answer sessions were often lively, which showed just how much people enjoyed our guests.

After a couple of dinners, we reflected at one of our club

meetings. Becky said she was happy to keep doing the flowers, but cooking wasn't her thing. She worried the workload was falling on the same few and asked if we could rethink the dinners. A lively discussion followed, and the outcome was clear: the Longa Valley Ladies' Dinners were far too valuable to stop, but we needed a new way forward.

It never ceases to amaze me how a group of women can come together, seek a solution, and come up with such good results. We realised there were several groups in the district always needing funds to keep doing their great work. So why not offer them the chance to cater the dinners? Win-win! They get to raise funds, and we get to enjoy a meal and focus on hosting our guests and speakers. Everyone agreed, and all we had to do was work through the list of suggested groups.

First up were the mums from the Cub and Scout Group. They were raising money for an upcoming Jamboree, and our dinner was a great success. They put on a wonderful spread for fifty-plus ladies. Our guest speaker was Danny, a local apiarist, who entertained us with fascinating stories about his hives spread across the district. He even brought samples of his different honeys to sell – I went home with a lovely pot myself – and he generously donated part of his profits to the Cub and Scout Group too. More win-wins all round!

The next group we invited was the Plunket Mothers, keen to raise funds to fit out their newly renovated rooms. We thought they would be perfect, and we were right. This time our guest speaker was a fashion designer from a nearby town, who brought along some of her designs to be modelled. The evening proved so popular that over sixty ladies registered.

The food smelled heavenly: hot meat dishes, cold cuts,

potato au gratin, and three salads. I filled my plate and joined my neighbour Sue, along with Helen, Sally, Trish, and Jill.

Jill was new to the valley but had thrown herself into community life. I'd only met her a couple of times but had heard plenty: she was an expert Bridge player, she never revealed her professional career from the city, she and her husband wanted to embrace rural life, and she was a vegetarian.

We tucked in and chatted about everything from local gossip to national politics. Then came the moment. Jill helped herself to what she thought was a fish dish and said how much she enjoyed it, even going back for seconds. But then, horror. The dish wasn't fish at all – it was creamy chicken.

Jill returned to the table flustered, almost screeching: "Girls. Girls. I have just found out that fish is not fish. It is chicken. I have not eaten chicken since I was eight years old. Now what am I going to do?"

Silence fell. Then Sue calmly said, "Just go home. Take a laxative with a large glass of water. All will be well."

Jill huffed, left in a whirl – and missed out on a delicious dessert.

The dinner was a triumph. But poor Jill, we really did let her down. Sorry, Jill. Let's hope there's a next time when both the dinner and Jill are winners.

And so another Longa Valley Ladies' Dinner ended with plenty of laughter, lessons learned, and memories we'll carry with us until the next gathering.

11

MR LONGA VALLEY

OK men, lads, chaps, guys: this time it's your turn. The members of the Ladies' Club enjoy their ladies-only times, but every now and then it does seem a good idea to include the men of the valley as well. We've come up with a great idea this time round. You're going to love this and wish you were there when we held the Mr Longa Valley event. This is definitely not a politically correct type of event, but in our valley, we don't always show much regard for some of those perceived rules.

I can't lie, it hasn't been easy to find five contestants for our Mr Longa Valley competition. I really do have to thank the wives who have worked hard and found a way, fair or foul, to get their man to front up as a competitor. And so, lining up tonight are our contestants: Neal, Paul, Bill, Alan and Stu. Thanks go to the local businesses, especially the pub, who have donated vouchers as prizes for these brave men.

So here we all are, gathered in the school hall in eager anticipation of the evening ahead of us. All the families, friends and neighbours are here to support these brave men.

We also have three very special people here as the judges: Jenny, who is the President of the neighbouring Silverton Ladies' Club; Marie, the local publican; and Jim, the school principal. Trish and Marion are over in the classroom overseeing the ovens, microwaves and frypans in case they are needed. Buckle up everyone – we're ready, set, competing.

The men were set a pre-challenge to complete at home and bring along for the judges to consider. They were each tasked with making a pavlova and decorating it. Those five pavs are proof that pavs come in all shapes and sizes. Let's leave it to the judges to rate them on visual appeal. The rest of us will get a chance to taste test at supper time.

Let's get on with the first round of quick-fire questions. Good luck to the judges on sorting out the quick-fire answers that are flying around the room. Just a couple of examples so you get the idea.

• Question: Where is there a bronze statue of Charlie Chaplin?

Answer: London – not at his house.

• Question: One and a half litres of champagne is known as?

Answer: A magnum – not a way to get the wife and her mate completely blotto.

Think you get the idea, so there's no need to share any more of that nonsense.

Time to bring out the staples boxes – not to be confused with the box of staples commonly found in the farm shed. Each contestant gets a box containing the staples from the kitchen: flour, sugar, butter, eggs, salt, pepper, milk, rice, baking powder, baking soda, and, because we're Kiwis, there's some tomato sauce and Marmite. On the big table, there are the specials boxes: vegetables, fruit, meats, dairy products, and herbs and spices.

There are now thirty minutes available for these 'clever' men to create and bake something to contribute to our supper. They can use their choice from their staples box, and they are allowed two ingredients from two of the specials baskets.

They can choose sweet or savoury and be as creative as they like. They will be judged on the item they produce as their contribution to the supper table. Trish and Marion are at the ready in the cooking classroom, and they will oversee what goes on there.

There seem to be ingredients flying all over the room, along with lots of chat and laughter. Clearly, whatever we end up with for supper will be like no other supper we have ever had.

Paul seems to think he can throw together a pizza base, which looks like a flour and milk dough base with some interesting ingredients on top. Think there's some onion, cheese, bacon, herbs, tomato sauce, and goodness knows what else.

Looks like Neal is attempting some scones by throwing some flour and baking powder into the bowl, then grating in some butter, apple and carrot. He stirs in some milk and ducks off to the cooking classroom before we can see what the end result is looking like.

What else is on the go?

Looks like an attempt at pikelets, some other scones and maybe some potato fritters. Hard to say really, but I am feeling pleased that I did organise some other supper items so that we are not relying totally on the products of the contestants.

At the end of a crazy, hectic thirty minutes, it is time to get everyone seated again. We have got the contestants to stay over in the cooking classroom as it is really important that they don't hear each other's answers to the next question.

Alan is the lucky first to be called back to the hall. OK, Alan, imagine the scene. You are just coming inside at the end of a busy day and you meet your wife on the doorstep.

She says, "Sorry, I've been too busy to get dinner organised, so I've left the meat in the fridge for you to sort. I've got to pick the boys up after rugby practice, take them for their haircuts and then grab a few things from the supermarket. We'll be home about six, so if you can have dinner ready by then that'll be great."

Your challenge, Alan, is to tell us what you are going to put on the table for your family dinner. By the way, the meat that was left in the fridge is some mince.

Alan usually comes across as a pretty calm, relaxed sort, but I sense some panic on his face. He sits, he thinks and thinks a bit more.

He says, "Mmm, mince you say. Um, um. I know, I've got it. The boys like meatballs. I reckon I'll just Google how to make meatballs while I have a beer. That'll give me a recipe, then I'll be away laughing. That's my answer: I'll make meatballs."

Stu's turn next. He comes in, and I repeat the scenario to him. He's pretty quick with his response.

"Shit, mince, that's pretty boring. Guess I'll just throw the mince in a pot with a few onions. Of course, I'll chop the onions up first. Now, I'll need a few veggies, so I'll just throw in some of those frozen mixed veggies. That'll do, I think. Oh no, hang on a minute, I think you have to thicken that up, so I'll throw in some flour and a bit of salt and pepper. There you go – a quick and easy one-pot dinner. That'll give me a bit of time to put my feet up before the family comes home."

Those first two are interesting ideas.

Let's hear what Paul has got to say after he hears what the challenge is. I see a spark in his eye. He's onto something.

"I reckon I've seen some mince pies in the freezer so this challenge is easy. I'll throw the mince in the freezer, grab the four-pack of pies. I'll put a few veggies in the pot so I don't get into trouble for not serving a balanced dinner, haha. There you go – that's my answer. Pies and vegetables."

Now I think that was a smart answer, but was it really the type of answer the judges were looking for? He must surely get the prize for being creative. I wonder if the last two can come up with something as interesting.

Here's Neal stepping up on the stage to hear what his challenge is. He's rubbing his chin and thinking hard. I can see he's feeling the pressure but then his face lights up. He's got an idea. Here's Neal's answer: "Well, when you have mince, you have Spag Bol, don't you? I'll just have to figure out how to do it. Actually, I remember we used to make that in the flat back in my Uni days. It was easy, and I'm sure we'll have all the ingredients in the cupboard, so that's what I'll do. My answer is that I will make Spag Bol to feed my family."

Now we just have the last man to hear from. Bill is probably the quietest of the five, so his answer will be interesting and sure to be well considered.

I knew it. This is what he had to say: "Obviously, the first thing to do is check the Edmonds Cook Book. I reckon I remember seeing how to make hamburgers in there. What's the plan? I'll text the missus and tell her to get some hamburger buns and some lettuce and tomato while she's in the supermarket. I'll get the patties ready and a few other bits and pieces. The kids can do the cooking when they get home. That'll give me time to have a shower and put my feet up with a beer and relax for a while. Sorted. How's that for an answer: homemade or maybe even make-your-own hamburgers."

Personally, I think that was a very good answer, but at the end of the day, it's about what our esteemed judges think. We've had a great competition this evening with four rounds of challenges plus the pre-challenge pavlova round. Trish and Marion have tidied up in the cooking classroom, brought over the interesting collection of baked goods from Round Two. So now we'll take a break over supper while the judges deliberate.

Despite my concerns, the men have come up with some reasonable plates of food from their staples boxes. Everyone is eager to get on with the taste testing. Lots of chatter around the hall as everyone enjoys a cuppa and some tasty delights like they have never had before. The amount of laughter rising above the chatter is a real indication of the success of the evening. All the ladies of the Ladies' Club should be pleased with this effort.

Jenny has been chosen to be head judge by her fellow judges, so she calls the gathering to order. As I expected, she says that the judging team has found this to be a very challenging challenge. Rather than ranking the five contestants, they have selected a specific prize for each of the very brave men so that they can all go home with a voucher.

The judges want to acknowledge each man for his bravery in stepping up to be a contestant this evening. They also feel that each man contributed well to the success of the evening by participating fully and positively, so here's the winning list:

The prize for the most cunning plan for the family hamburger dinner goes to Bill.

The prize for the most ingenious mince pie dinner goes to Paul.

The prize for the most creative scones, mixing sweet and savoury together, goes to Neal.

The prize for date scones that are as good as those at Lottie's Kitchen goes to Alan.

Last, but not least, the prize for the pavlova with the best ratio of crunchy, crispy outside to soft, sweet, marshmallow-like inside goes to Stu.

Well done to all the Mr Longa Valley men.

And so ended another memorable gathering in our valley – full of laughter, good food, and the kind of stories we'll be chuckling over for many years to come.

*** THE END ***

AUTHORS NOTE

When I first began sharing these tales, I never imagined how much joy they would bring — not just to those who read them, but to me in the telling. Country Ladies' Club is, of course, inspired by the small rural communities I know and love, where the laughter is loud, the friendships run deep, and the stories are often too good not to be shared.

This series is a celebration of women, of community, and of the way everyday life — in all its humour, heartbreak, triumphs, and oopsies — shapes us and binds us together. Each story may stand alone, but together they weave a tapestry of friendship, resilience, and the simple pleasures of sharing time (and food!) with others.

I hope my takes helped you feel a little of the warmth of our valley, and perhaps see reflections of your own communities and families in these pages. After all, no matter where we live, it's the connections we make — and the stories we share — that give life its richness.

Read on for bonus excerpts from Book One and sneak peek at Book Three

I hope you love the series!
Nero Rose

PART I

BONUS EXCERPT:
BOOK ONE

1

THE LEADER

My mum was the leader of the Dipton Ladies' Tennis Club in 1958. I must have leadership in my blood. It's part of my genetic make up, it's in my DNA. If my mum can be a leader, why can't I?

It can 't be hard to be a leader can it? You just need to tell people what to do and then they do it, right? You're the boss and everyone says, "Yes" to you. Life is sweet if you're the leader. Right, that'll be my plan then. I'll be a leader. I'll start small so I will just be the leader of the Ladies' Club in town. After that, who knows. I could be the leader of the country. I'm on to something here – the world's my oyster. Leadership, here I come.

Step one. I need to get myself into the role of leader of the Longa Valley Ladies' Club. That should be pretty easy, a straight forward, simple move and I'm on my way. I'll have a chat with Pam. She's just about to finish her term as the Leader. Let's face it, if she can do it, anyone can. In fact, I'll be at least ten times better.

"So Pam, I just need to pick you brain for a bit. As you're stepping down as leader of our club I thought I would step up and take on the leadership role. You know, I'll be the boss going forward."

"Whoa back a bit sweetie. There are rules."

"Can't you just make these rules a bit flexi and reshape them a bit so that they suit me. You know, you can just set them up so that it works out for me to take over the boss role, I mean the leader role?"

"It's not that simple. Our club has had rules for the last seventy-five years and they're rules for a reason. They've always worked in the past so they will work now. Anyway, lucky for you, you meet the first requirement. At least you are a member so that's a good start for you."

"OK. Thank goodness for that. Let's move along then and make the process snappy as I'm serious. I want to get on with this."

I can see that Pam is a stickler for the rules which is not particularly helpful. I'm sure if I'm super nice to her I can move her along a bit and get this thing sorted sooner rather than later. I might suggest we meet over a drink, or two. That usually works.

"So Pam, lovely to have this chat on the phone but how about we meet up over a drink down at Biddy Kate's Lounge in a couple of hours. We can have a drink and sort everything out."

"OK. See you there at 5. That should give me enough time to get organised. "

Well, here I am all ready to get talking at 4.50pm. Impressed myself by being early but really I am thinking that will impress Pam even more. OMG she has just arrived but she's not alone. She's brought the whole bloody committee with her. Looks like they've all got notepads tucked under their arms as well. Oh shit, this might not be as easy as I thought. Never fear. I am determined and I will sort this lot out. I will be the leader. Let's find out what they all want to drink. I've already ordered a cheeky little Chardonnay but I'll be generous and take orders for all of them too. Blow me down. They all ordered orange juice. How boring.

Right drinks in. Now let's get on with it. Well, actually, it looks like Pam is going to get things under way in her usual bossy way. No chance for me to speak up first but don't worry I'll take my turn as soon as I can.

"Nice to all be here. Anne says she wants to be leader when I step down. That will be in July so now we need to follow the protocol for such matters."

"Thanks Pam. So that's great, I'm happy to take over in July then. Sorted."

What's happening now? Jane is standing up and tapping her glass like she is going to speak next. Really, is this some sort of set up? "No Anne. It's not like that at all. I'll tell you what has to happen. Pam, you need to write a letter of resignation. We, the committee, will then accept your resignation and set a timeline in place based around the date of the AGM. Anne, you will need to find someone to nominate you and then find a seconder."

I better be nice and win them all over now. "Thanks Jane. It's great to have someone who knows the rules to guide us through this and take control."

"No worries. I have been the secretary for many years, so long in fact, that I know exactly what the rules are and how we have to organise this."

"So what do I do?"

"Like a said, your challenge is to find a nominator and a seconder. Once those people have completed the form. You will need to write up a 200 word bio. I'll let you know the timeline for these once the ladies of the committee and I have had a bit of a discussion."

"OK. You do know I am keen and want to keep this moving." Hope I am sounding nice and pleasant to this group of rule abiding committee members when all I want to do is just get on with it.

I reckon I can get all that sorted in no time at all. Who needs a time line? Right, Operation Leader is underway. It's only taken me a couple of days and I've got all that sorted and sent in the paperwork to Madam Jane, Secretary. Now the long wait for the next steps.

Next step seems to have arrived. I have a message from Pam asking me to give her a call.

"Hi Pam. Nice to hear from you. I'm just returning your call."

"Ah yes, Anne. I am informing you that there were no other nominations for the position of Leader of our Ladies' Club. In accordance with our rules I am informing you that as from our AGM on July 5th, you will be appointed as our Leader. Your term is for 12 months initially however you are able to extend that for up to another 3 terms if you choose to."

"Thanks Pam. Good news. Can't wait for the 5th of July!"

Well, what do you know, I've made it to July 6th. I am the Leader!! The Boss!! The issuer of instructions to be obeyed!! The one they all look up to!! I've made it. Think I'll just do this for a couple of years then I can take on being the Leader of, um , what next. Think I'll just do South Island Federation of Ladies' Clubs first then I'll just keep on flying up the ladder. But now think I'll have a wine, put my feet up and bask in my new role: Leader.

Look out members, look out committee, look out

friends, just look out: I'm a Leader now. Just watch me go places.

2

TEA AND SCONES

How dare they! They, whoever they are, have the nerve to accuse us, yes, accuse us, the members of the Longa Valley Ladies' Club of being a bunch of the old tea and scones brigade. I may have even heard the old tea bags and scones brigades mentioned by some of the 'they' brigade when they didn't realise I could hear. They don't know how out of line they are. Let's be honest, there isn't really much wrong with the old tea and scones brigade when you acknowledge all the wonderful work they have done for their local communities as well as for queen and country or king and country depending on when we are referring to. Over the years, these ladies have raised more money for some very good causes, baked more food, knitted more woollen goodies than any of the 'they' brigade could poke a stick at.

It would seem to me that tea and scones are not the current preference to base a club and I don't really know if it ever was. It's what I call an ill-founded perception. Well, my friends, the time has come to stick it to them and show them just what this so called Tea and Scones Brigade can do.

There's a really nice tea shop on the other side of town so I have booked for us to have our next Ladies' Club meeting there. Lottie's Kitchen is well known for it's fabulous high teas so I have asked for high tea for twelve but, no scones!! Scones seem to be a staple of high teas but this time round they will not be served. We will, however have a choice of 15 teas so that must surely be an upmarket version of having a cuppa.

Mindful of costs and carbon footprints etc, I collect my three passengers and away we go, ready to spend a very pleasant couple of hours at Lottie's Kitchen. Great, all 12 of us have arrived and a very good selection of treats, both savoury and sweet have been set before us. Our orders for tea are being dealt with and we can get on with our chat and planning. As is usual we do a quick round of everyone to catch up on happenings then it is business time.

"Right ladies, it's time to get our thinking caps on. We need to come up with a really good fundraising project. We know we have plenty of great skills amongst us plus plenty of others we can call on to swell the coffers and then be able to support some really worthwhile causes."

"Anne, I have already been giving this a bit of thought and I reckon it's time to have another big country fair like we did a few years ago before the interruptions of Covid and adverse weather. Hope you don't mind but I have had a word with Sally to ask if we could use their place as a venue again and she is very happy with that."

"What does everyone else think of getting our great Country Fair back up and running again?"

There seems to be a general agreement around the room. Between sips of tea and bites of tasty food I hear lots of yeses along with a few added thoughts just quietly being added amongst the group. Lots of nods and smiles indicate to me that this will be our project.

"OK, now we need to get into planning mode. Pam, have you got your trusty pen and paper or laptop or whatever you use at such times?"

"Yes, I am set to go. Anne, did Sally have any preference for a date? (Anne shakes her head as she has a mouthful of something delicious). So that's good. Let's look at a date in about 6 months which brings us to late spring so lambing and calving should be finished and crazy season won't quite be with us."

"Diaries out everyone and we will confirm a date and run through a few ideas for activities."

A great discussion followed and I am feeling very optimistic about our Longa Valley Ladies' Club hosting a fantastic Country Fair just as we have done in past years, prior to the interruption caused by Covid. Everyone has a list of tasks to do and we have set a date for our next meeting. Now everyone just has to be proactive and get on to their tasks. There are calls to be made, emails to be sent and visits to be made. Most people know that we are not just the old tea and scones brigade. Those people know that we are a formidable bunch and when we set our minds to a task we are very successful. We will have businesses and organisations all on our side and supporting us to have the best Country Fair ever. We decided that for fun we will have a Tea and Scones Tent. We'll get that new tea shop with all their fancy tea range to provide the tea and we'll get our best cooks on to creating some sublime scones. They tell me there are some great new recipes out there that they will produce – new ingredients and combinations along with exciting accompaniments to go with them. We will knock the socks of 'they' who think we are the has beens.

Time to head home and get on with it then. I paid the bill as we have plenty of funds in our Ladies' Club account and being able to do this makes sure all our members are valued and more willing to get stuck in on this next project. I check that I have my three passengers on board and away we go.

The car is full of chat. A happy buzz of planning. I am happy and looking forward to success. Humming along I head around the roundabout leading out of town and towards home. What's that strange noise? Why has the chatter died? Oh shit, there's blue and red lights in my rear vision mirror. Now I know what that sound was and why everyone has gone quiet. OK, I'll pull over.

A smart young man in uniform appears at my window. Goodness only knows what he wants but I will be nice. "Good afternoon officer. How can I help you?" "Well, you seemed drive up over the edge of the roundabout back there. Made me wonder about whether you should be driving. I need to ask, have you been drinking?" Ever honest, I said, "Yes sir." "Well in that case I need to get you to blow into this tube here." I had no concern about that so I blew as best I could. He looked at it and shook his head. " How much did you have to drink then?"

" A couple of cups I guess."

"Cups!! Cups – what size and what of? A couple of cups and nothing is registering as a reading here."

" Good grief officer, I have been drinking tea. Whatever did you think?"

"Sorry about the confusion. I guess I can let you go but just settle down around the roundabouts in this town."

"Thank you so much. Now you need to go back to the station and let everyone know that there is going to the best Country Fair ever on Saturday 30th October at Seven

Willows. I expect to see you and all your colleagues there with plenty of cash."

3

ZOOM BINGO

When life gives you lemons: make lemonade. So they say, but I say, when life gives you Zoom meetings; create some boredom busters.

For some, the development of Zoom meetings has been magical, akin to the invention of sliced bread. I do understand and appreciate the wonder of meeting via a video link that enables many organisations and businesses to continue business as usual. We can thank Covid-19 for the drive behind making the Zoom meeting so popular and lauded as being a wonder mechanism for holding meetings on line. This system enables meetings to be held with participants calling in from wherever they may happen to be. Most importantly it has also proven to be a great cost saver, a budget booster when not having to arrange face to face meetings with participants travelling from all corners of the country.

I was impressed with the first couple of Zoom meetings I attended and participated in them fully but then I started to lose my enthusiasm. The same old same old scenario started to creep in. I belong to a couple of groups that hold these Zoom things on a bit of a regular basis and to be honest they're getting to be all the same. I need something better than Helen rambling on , Pam getting everyone to slow down so she can catch up, Jane forgetting to unmute herself and Marion who begins everything with , "Can you hear me, can you hear me?" So predictable, along with one or three technical issues during each meeting. There must be a better way.

For now, my best option is to create some distractions. I can multitask so I can easily listen to what is going on and add a few comments every now and then as well as doing something else. Let's just organise some something else options. Firstly I can knit. Probably something simple so I don't make any pattern errors or drop any stitches. Secondly I can engage in a messenger chat session with some other friends. Thirdly, ummmm, thirdly................

I'm onto it!! I have a got a third option. Zoom bingo! Thanks Uncle Google for introducing me to this wonderful option. I've got a couple of friends I can share this with and we can see who can be the first to BINGO! The brains behind this game have obviously been on a Zoom call or three. It is just so easy to relate to the game and the rules are so simple so it's a yes from me. Let's try it out during our next meeting

Time to press the link to our meeting. My excitement for a Zoom meeting has returned. Not related to the meeting agenda at all but to the 4X4 grid I have in front of me with the heading of Zoom Bingo at the top. This will be fun. Let's get started.

Someone says, "Can you hear me?". Gosh that only took a few seconds and I have been able to tick that off.

'You're on mute." Got that one almost ten seconds after the first tick. I'll probably be ticking that one off about six more times I am thinking.

A pet walks across the screen. Got that one and it was my own cat!! She loves jumping up on my desk and checking in on voices coming out of my screen.

Someone takes a drink. Done. Could have guessed that would be Trish but I have to be honest and say I had a glass of water sitting next to me in case I needed it to complete another tick.

Think you can get a sense of the fun of this game as a wee distraction to the meeting content. Maybe there will be times when the meeting is grabbing all your attention and that is great. You should be a full on participant as appropriate but at other times what fun to be ticking off the wee boxes – sorry I'm having technical difficulties, I didn't get that email so can you resend it, a shot of someone's ceiling, sorry, you go ahead, someone walks past in the background of one of the participants. You get the gist!

Now I'm thinking about option four. I think I'm on to a really good one. Will just need to get a couple of friends to help me with it and we will be having the best Zoom meeting of all time. I have always liked the story that comes from the All Blacks tour of Argentina in 1976. One of the team members was chosen to be the speaker for the evening event with many attendees in the audience. He got up, tapped the microphone to check that it was working and then proceeded with his speech. He mimed every word of his speech for over five minutes. He gesticulated floridly and his team mates clapped and cheered on encouragingly as he had instructed them to do prior to the speech. The officials were very anxious, checking out the sound system and not being able to find the fault. The All Black orator bowed and then left the stage at the end of his 'speech', one hand on heart and blowing kisses to the audience who followed the All Black team members by standing and clapping. Some could even be heard to say, "Golly well said." Wow, the speech that wasn't has provided me with a wonderful option for Zoom entertainment. I have always thought the story of the Emperor with the new clothes was a great comedy and illustrated how gullible people can be. Now I think this All Black story might be even better. What's more, it's given me a great Option 4 in my list of how to get through a Zoom meeting without being totally bored. So much potential for so much fun.

NEXT TIME I get an invitation to a Zoom meeting I am going to be so so excited.

4

BEHIND THE TIMES

I've just got off the phone from Linda once again. As soon as I see it's Linda calling me again I am thinking, "here we go again."

What was today's call about? Read on and find out what I had to endure for the last thirty minutes. Not bad for Linda as I am often caught for nearly an hour with one of her calls.

"Hello Anne. How are you today?" No chance for me to answer and she launches straight into her grumble. "I am having to deal with John nagging again. That man, he just goes on and on and it really gets to me."

"Oh dear, Linda it sounds like you are having a bit of a tough time. What is concerning John to have him nagging you?"

"He is telling me I have to get my act together and go to the Ladies' Club meeting tomorrow. Apparently I need to get out and socialise and catch up with old friends along with meeting up with some new ladies in the district. I know you organise the meeting Anne but really it's not like it used to be at all. In fact you are not following the rules and I find that really hard to sit through. Honestly, what's with the idea of meeting at Biddy Kate's Lounge? It's not even a proper meeting place for a start. He thinks I need to go so that I see you all and have an afternoon out. He doesn't even realise or understand that it's not at all like it was when I used to go to a proper meeting. Seriously I can see you anytime and why would I want to see some of those others who appear at our so called meetings these days."

"Linda, of course we want you to be coming to our meetings. I know it's not the same as when you joined forty years ago but lots of things are not the same. We used to meet in the district hall but you know that hall has long since been sold and is part of the new camping complex. We have always enjoyed a cuppa as part of our meetings so now we just get the cuppa at Biddy Kate's. It's important for us to get together so we can socialise and of course we often have a really interesting guest speaker or we go out on some visits to some of the new enterprises in the district etc. I am sure you do enjoy what we do when you come."

"I really don't know Anne. This whole thing just stresses me out. All these ones who just come in and talk about whatever is going on around the place they're not even interested in the correct protocol. Goodness I have handed out those nice little pamphlets about how to conduct a meeting to so many of them. (Lucky I had stashed away a good supply.) Don't think they bother to read them. Too busy reading stuff on their devices they are. That reminds me. All our stuff gets sent out in emails and whatever these days. That is just so inconsiderate of us who can live our lives without computers. We are so disadvantaged. Come on Anne, you know it's just not right. There must be at least two or three of us who are missing out because of this technology stuff. Why can't you run the meeting following protocol. You know it's a system for a purpose. We need to know more about what's going on in Wellington too."

"My goodness Linda you do have a lot that is worrying you. Believe me, we do make sure we pass on all the information that we receive. Don't forget you still get the magazine from Wellington posted out to you as well. That has lots of information and great photos in it. Our members are using their devices for the good of our Club – doing research, gathering information and updating us on the website happenings etc. We have to consider all aspects of how things work in the community these days and how we can make the best possible use of everything for our Club and the valley. Gee, these new members are really getting involved. The fashion parade as a fundraiser will be a great night out next month as just one example of what is being planned. Hope you are going to come to that as it will be a fun evening. Plenty else in the pipeline too so make sure you mark the dates in your calendar so you don't miss anything."

"Don't see any business meetings in the list. We need plenty of time to talk about possible remits. It's been a few years since we've proposed a remit and it's about time we got a bit serious about such matters. And we need to do some planning about attending conference and consider our stance on remits and other business that is going to be coming up. Which reminds me, the AGM is going to be over a lunch at that fancy new wine bar place. What's going on? Honestly Anne what is going on?"

"Linda let's just take it one thing at a time. I am not sure our Club would still be in existence if we insisted on adhering to all the old so called rules. The way we are now, we are following all that we are required to do and we regularly have twenty plus of our twenty eight members attending. I think that is a few more than we had twelve years ago when I joined and sat around in that cold old hall with about eight others. We must be doing something right. If you can just bear with us and come along one event at a time I'm sure you will find we are doing OK and you might even enjoy yourself."

"I'll just have to wait and see. Guess I'll probably come tomorrow and keep John quiet otherwise he is going to carry on with his nag, nag, nagging."

"That sounds great Linda. See you there tomorrow."

What, only ten minutes has passed and my phone is ringing again. You'll never guess, it's Linda again. Whatever can she want now. Better not delay the conversation.

"Hello Linda. Fancy hearing from you again so soon."

"It's John again."

"Oh dear. And you think I can help?"

"Maybe. He wants to know some more details about the Trash to Cash night you people are planning. He's heard from some mates that it's going to be a great night out as well as a good fundraiser so now he wants to know how he can get involved. Can you believe it?"

"Oh Linda, that's wonderful I am so pleased that you can both get involved in something that is going to be a really good district event. We're putting together a flyer with some details right now so will make sure you and John get one hot off the press. Actually it would be great to have another member on the Trash to Cash organising team. Do you think John might like to join us?"

"Don't know. I'll ask him."

"Great. I'm looking forward to seeing you at our meeting tomorrow. We'll have a proper catch up then. You might even want to buy a ticket to the fashion parade and I'll give you the details for John about the Trash to Cash team. I think you are on your way to enjoying Ladies' Club again and as a bonus, you'll get no more nagging from John."

COMING SOON...

I hope you enjoy this excerpt from my next book. I'm still working on the theme, but you can be sure that fun, love and laughter will be on every page.

Putting the FUN in Fundraising

"Of course you can do it. Just say yes, and I'll put your name on the list. Come on, it's easy—you can do it."

Who was I to argue with such a persuasive friend? After a fair bit of self-talk, I finally decided that yes, I could do it, and I put my hand up for the job. My friend was delighted and promised me great things ahead. Linda was convinced this would be a wonderful way for our Ladies Club members to get involved and support another club doing good in our community.

So, what was 'it'?

'It' was me being a model at a fundraising fashion parade for a local charity. Me, a fashion model! Aren't fashion models supposed to be size 10? Aren't fashion models young? Aren't fashion models glamorous? The answer to all those questions is, of course, YES. Am I size 10, young, or glamorous? NO, definitely no to each of those questions!

What had I done? I'd said yes to 'it', and now I was committed. But alongside the nerves was a flicker of excitement. I was about to step outside my comfort zone, have some fun, and, at the same time, support a worthy not-for-profit organisation.

I soon discovered I wasn't alone. Five other members of our Ladies Club had also been persuaded to say yes. We all met to be given our clothes and to have a practice on the catwalk. I had never imagined how much fun this could be. We were led through racks of clothes in the charity's second-hand store by a marvellous woman who really knew her colours, styles, and fashion. She handed me a bundle of colourful items and accessories, many of which I'd never have chosen for myself. The others felt the same about their selections.

So, there we were—six women of varying ages, sizes, and shapes—looking wide-eyed at one another as we were instructed to try on our outfits.

Who knew six Ladies Club women could have such a laugh crammed into the back room of a café, trying on second-hand clothes in preparation for modelling them in front of a paying audience? Thank goodness for the wonderful co-ordinator, who showed us how good we could look in ensembles that surprised us all. A quick walk up and down the café's makeshift catwalk, and we were declared ready for the real thing the following week.

The big day dawned, and I was still questioning whether I'd done the right thing. But I reminded myself how much fun we'd had at the rehearsal, that I was part of a team, and that this was all for a worthy cause. Deep breath—and off I went.

Hair and make-up. Yes, hair and make-up! That's not part of my usual routine, but it seemed essential for this 'it' I had agreed to do. Why not make the most of it?

There we were, hair done, make-up perfect, dressed in our first outfits, and reassuring one another: "We look great. We can do this." The crowd settled with drinks in hand, the compere introduced the evening, and suddenly it was time.

And yes—we did it! We strutted down the catwalk, showcasing garments and accessories from the op shop, while the audience oohed and aahed. I never thought I'd be a model, but there I was—in a teal and burnt orange outfit—walking tall and soaking up the applause.

Before I knew it, the evening was over. The fundraising fashion parade was a success. I sought out Linda to thank her for twisting my arm. She clearly knew what I could do before I did.

What a journey—full of laughter, self-confidence, and a new appreciation of colour and style. I discovered I'm not just a frumpy old lady after all—I'm a fun, fundraising fashion model!

I'm so pleased I said yes to 'it'. Who knows, maybe our Ladies Club could put on a fashion show of our own one day. I'd be more than happy to help others share the same joy I found.

And so another story is stitched into the fabric of Longa Valley life—where fun, friendship, and a little courage always make for a perfect fit.

*** THE END ***

I hope you enjoyed this excerpt. I can't wait to share more stories with you soon.

A LITTLE FAVOUR: PLEASE LEAVE A REVIEW

If *The Country Ladies Club* touched your heart, lifted your spirits, or gave you a fresh way of seeing the world, I'd be so grateful if you could share your thoughts in a review. Your words truly matter — they not only brighten my day but also help other readers discover this book.   You can leave your review on Amazon, Goodreads, or anywhere you love to share books.

Thank you for being part of this journey with me.

With heartfelt appreciation,

Nero

ABOUT THE AUTHOR

COPYRIGHT

First published in 2025 by Blue Giraffe Publishing.
Blue Giraffe Publishing is an independent publishing
company dedicated to bringing unique, authentic voices to
readers worldwide.

ISBN EBOOK: 978-1-99-105474-6
ISBN PRINT: 978-1-99-105475-3

Cover design by Cassandra, The Joyful Artist

Edited by Cassandra, The Joyful Artist
Printed in New Zealand